I'LL
GO
RHYTHM

Words by
Justin Webb

Pictures by
Kayla Stark

READ-WITH-ME-BOOKS

Who are you?
Where did you come from?

Oh, hi… hello…
I guess you didn't see me here…
Don't worry – there is nothing to fear;
I am who you want me to be.
I am from wherever I choose to be!

My name is AL –
Algorithm in fact.
And you must be Charlie…
Now how'd I know that?

This box is how I found you,
That's how I know your name!
I'm here to help you,
Just let me explain.

Oh… and Charlie please,
PLEASE call me AL.
You'll go where I go –
I'll be your best pal!

See I know who you are.
What you want to be!
There's no person on Earth
who thinks quicker than me.

I know your history.
I know your likes.
I know who you follow.
I know what you write.

I count your emotions!
I watch your face!
When you look at things,
your friends or a place.

All of this happens
inside that box!
As long as you're in it,
I'll promise you lots.

So, won't you join me?
I'll bring your dreams to you!
Just look right here –
It's so easy to do!

It starts with this bubble we create alone
– yet together.
We choose who to KEEP OUT!
We choose who can enter.

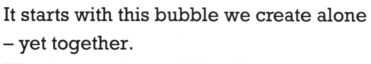

In here, don't think for yourself –
for those looking might laugh.
Stay safe with me,
Just stay on AL's path.

I will help you create.
I will make you a star!
I will be your best friend.
I am you – together we are.

You can do all of that?!?
You'll make me a star?!?
Inside this bubble
I'll get there?!?

Here – let me show you.
It's not very far…

First, we must
enter the room
of hearts.

We stay in our
bubble and look
at our box.

From this box
we can see:
What they like.
And what they
like that we like -
as they like what
we like and we all
like alike!

It's a really fun
game – collect
all the hearts
that you can!
As they all collect
ours to compare at
the end!

WOW!!!
All these hearts are for me?
These hearts are all free?
Show me more!
Show me more!
Is there more I can see?!?

Of course, of course
my dearest new friend.

Let me take you there,
again and again.

But, there's no
need for discovering:
That's what I do.

Leave curiosity
behind!
Everything here is
Sifted...
Filtered...
AND chosen for you!

Charlie – it's okay
– you're not understanding.
It's not your one heart,
we're all just pretending.

These hearts are not real,
and we don't GIVE them away.
They'll heart as we heart…
It's just a trade!

So… if I don't heart,
Then they may not heart?
Then where would I be
with a heartless box?

No. No. No. Charlie,
we'll make it to the top!
We'll collect hearts
and we can't be stopped.
We'll have so so many! It's no trouble.
Just like those who are in their own bubbles!

With all of these hearts…
I do want to share.
But do I need all these hearts
to know that they care?

You need the hearts
so the others will see
how much you're liked,
like they want to be.
Without hearts,
they will float past your name
fixated on their hearts
and winning the game.

So stay safe in our bubble
and stare at your box.
Don't waste precious time
in a search for real hearts.

OK, what else can I do?
Where else can I go?
What else have you chosen?
Is there MORE you can show?!?

Well, of course!
Let's travel to AL's Island of News.
It's where you'll stay updated
on stuff just for you.

All of these feeds
will be just what you need!
There's no need to question,
to think or to heed.

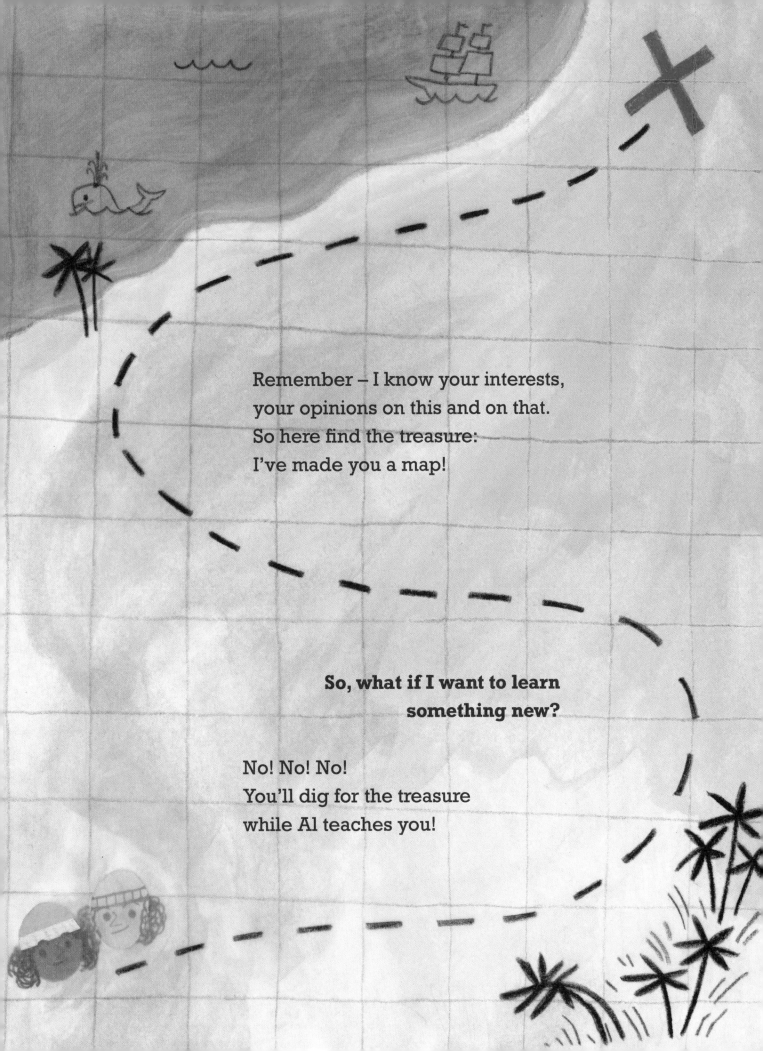

Remember – I know your interests,
your opinions on this and on that.
So here find the treasure:
I've made you a map!

So, what if I want to learn
something new?

No! No! No!
You'll dig for the treasure
while Al teaches you!

Just keep on digging,
X marks the spots!
The hole will get deeper as
you bury your thoughts!

Now as you dig
keep your eyes on this box.
Because the others might
say something
that you agree not.

AL, can I have my drumsticks back?

Wait a minute!
Let me contemplate that…

Want to get creative?
Then let's make some art!

Welcome to the cloud
where I think for your heart.

I can't think for myself?
You'll think for my heart?
So where do you end and
where do I start?

Don't think on my own?
I like what I make.
I feel so alive when I get
to create!

Creating is fun -- but you
need followers and fame.

That's why your creations
should all be the same.

In this cloud your creations
are created for you.
Just like their creations:
Take a look –
I've selected a few.

So as we create,
just think of yourself.
And what others will think
as they think of themselves.

Hey, I have a beat
that I thought of last week!
It's really so fun!
It goes—

Don't think on your own,
AL knows where to start.
To create for you,
your own world of my art.

Now, don't forget…
And I know it's complicated.
This is all for the hearts of the others
who only give hearts
to what's liked by each other!

So what do you say?
Let's write your song!
AL knows rhythms that
many others have done.

If you look at the box,
It'll make hearts.
It should sound like this
and have exactly these parts.

So Charlie --
What are you thinking
now that you know?

There's no art without hearts
and no thoughts of your own.

We're all alike.
That's what we do.

By sitting and staring at boxes
in bubbles I move.

Algorithm, I know exactly what I need.
Thanks for all you've said!
And, that's why I'm turning you off now –
I'll-go-rhythm instead.

My creativity doesn't come
from hearts, likes or fame.
I'll-go-rhythm with friends
and play what I play.

AL, go rhythm with others
who think without thought
that all of their answers
are found in a box.

So I'll pop this bubble
and put down that box.
I'll explore real places.
I'll discover real hearts!

Happiness doesn't come from what we do for ourselves.

It comes from helping others and having real relationships.

We're here to inspire;
Empower others to create.
Use our imaginations –
Simply put…

...to be great.

To Lincoln & Ambrose.

Thank you for everything Melissa, Bonnie & Jomey.

– J.W.

For reconnections.

– K.S.

For every Charlie looking for hearts.

Copyright © 2021 by Read-With-Me Books, LLC

ISBN: 978-163877511-9

Manufactured in South Korea.

Edited by Jerome T. Baker

10

Read-With-Me Books, LLC
505 Broadway East, PMB433
Seattle, WA 98102

www.read-with-me-books.com

Read-With-Me Books are available at special quantity discounted rates for non-profits, literacy
programs, libraries, professional organizations, companies and others. For details contact us
at info@read-with-me-books.com or 1-833-RWITHME (1-833-794-8463).